by Alison Inches
illustrated by Dave Aikins

Hi! I am Dora.

Do you like surprises?

Then follow me!

Hop across the rocks!

Hop! Hop! Hop!

Splash in the water!

Just like me!

Row across the lake!

Row! Row! Row!

Slide down the hill!

Just like me!

Are we there yet?

Not yet!

Swing on the vines!

Swing! Swing! Swing!

Jump over the logs!

Just like me!

Here we are!

Guess what we see!

An ice-cream party!

Yummy!

We did it!

I Love My Mami!

by Judy Katschke
illustrated by Dave Aikins

Hi! I am Dora!

I am going to spend
the day with my **mami**.

29

First we feed the babies.

Then we make a
yummy breakfast.

My **mami** takes me with her to work.

Look what I found!

Then **Mami** and I go to the park.

We play on the swings.
Higher and higher we go!

I made a present
for **Mami.**

It is a picture of us!

Mami and I
had a great day.

I love my **mami**!
And **Mami** loves me.

by Christine Ricci
illustrated by Robert Roper

Hi! I am .
DORA

Look! There is a
KITE

stuck in that .
TREE

We have to help her!

51

How can we reach
the top of the ?
TREE
I have a  in my .
ROPE   BACKPACK

We need the longest .
ROPE

Do you see it?

 is a great climber!
BOOTS

 rescued the  !
BOOTS   KITE

54

The has to get to
KITE

the 🌈 Festival
RAINBOW KITE

before the 🌈 disappears.
RAINBOW

Will you help us?

How do we get to

the  RAINBOW KITE Festival?

Let's ask MAP!

56

 says the   Festival is

MAP · RAINBOW KITE

at the top of Tallest .

MOUNTAIN

First we go past the .

WINDMILL

Then we go through   .

RAINBOW · DOOR

We made it to the  .

WINDMILL

It is so windy!

58

We need to turn off the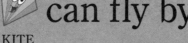

WINDMILL

so the can fly by.

KITE

But the is blowing us

WIND

away from the .

SWITCH

I know!

I need  to make a .
STRING   LASSO

Do you see any ?
STRING

The little has !
KITE   STRING

We lassoed the
SWITCH

and stopped the !
WIND

RAINBOW DOOR has **7** SEVEN LOCKS!

Can you find **7** SEVEN KEYS

to match the **7** SEVEN LOCKS?

Oh, no! I see .
SWIPER

He will try to swipe the .
KEYS

We have to stop him.

Say " , no swiping!"
SWIPER

63

We stopped !
SWIPER

The 7  opened
SEVEN KEYS

the 7  on   .
SEVEN LOCKS   RAINBOW   DOOR

Next comes Tallest .
MOUNTAIN

There it is!

We have to hurry!

The  is starting to fade!
RAINBOW

Tallest  MOUNTAIN is so tall!

How can we get to the top?

The can fly us

KITE

to the top of the .

MOUNTAIN

We can hold on to her !

RIBBONS

67

We made it to the

 Festival!

RAINBOW KITE

All of the are so happy.

KITES

But where is the ?

RAINBOW

Say "Come back, !"

RAINBOW

The  heard us

RAINBOW

and came back.

Look at his colors!

The  are ready to fly.

KITES

Here they go!

Look at all of the  **KITES**

flying under the  **RAINBOW**!

We did it!

Thanks for helping!

adapted by Molly Reisner
based on the original screenplay by Eric Weiner
illustrated by Susan Hall

Hi! I am .
DORA

This is my first time

exploring!

Will you come with me?

I see  !

FOOTPRINTS

I use my

MAGNIFYING GLASS

to follow the  .

FOOTPRINTS

Who is here?

It is a monkey who

wears  !
RED BOOTS

His name is  .
BOOTS

Hi,  ! My name is  .
BOOTS   DORA

Oh, no! A sneaky fox wants

to swipe the from !

RED BOOTS   BOOTS

The fox is named .

 and I say,

" , no swiping!"

We stopped !

and I meet the .

BOOTS   FIESTA TRIO

The will play music

FIESTA TRIO

for the on the .

QUEEN BEE   MOUNTAIN

The  does not like to
QUEEN BEE
wait!

Oh, no! The  dropped

FIESTA TRIO

their  !

INSTRUMENTS

Will you help us bring the

 to the  ? Great!

INSTRUMENTS   FIESTA TRIO

The 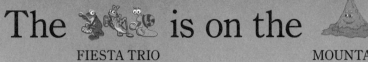 is on the .
FIESTA TRIO   MOUNTAIN

We need to go through

the 🌳.
FOREST

and across the 〰️.
RIVER

83

 are falling in the .

NUTS   FOREST

We need to move fast!

BOOTS sees his friend **TICO**.

TICO will drive us through

the **FOREST** in his **CAR**.

Now we have to follow the

's trail.

FIESTA TRIO   BIKE

The trail goes

BIKE

through a 🌳 .

TREE

Does the  trail go through

BIKE

the 🌳 or the 🌳 ?

CIRCLE TREE   TRIANGLE TREE

Yes! The 🌳.

CIRCLE TREE

We made it to the river.

This is  the iguana.
ISA

 wants to come
ISA

with us too.

We need a to cross
BOAT

the .
RIVER

 turns his into a !
TICO   CAR   BOAT

89

Which way do we go?

 knows!

ISA

We have to follow the

numbers **1**, **2**, and **3**.

ONE TWO THREE

Do you see **1**, **2**, and **3**?
ONE   TWO   THREE

Smart looking!

Oh, no! fell into the !
BOOTS RIVER

 the bull fishes
BENNY BOOTS

out of the .
RIVER

Thanks for helping, !
BENNY

Now we have to get to the top of the  .

MOUNTAIN

turns his into

TICO CAR

an .

AIRPLANE

We fly up, up, up!

We reached the top of

the .
MOUNTAIN

Here are your  , 🎷🐛🐌!
INSTRUMENTS   FIESTA TRIO

The can play
FIESTA TRIO

music now.

The  loves the music!
QUEEN BEE

Thanks for helping!
I love exploring and
meeting new friends!

NICKELODEON

DORA the EXPLORER

The Puppy Twins

adapted by Sarah Willson
based on the screenplay "Bark, Bark to Play Park"
written by Brian Bromberg
illustrated by Steve Savitsky

Hola! I am !
DORA

This is my friend .
BOOTS

This is my puppy, 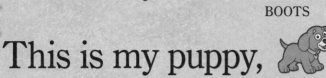.
PERRITO

We are going to a twin !
PARTY

99

is excited.

PERRITO

 has a twin.

PERRITO

's twin will be at the .

PERRITO   PARTY

100

We need to show us the

way to the party.

Look!

has a twin sister!

says that first

MAP

we must go to the

DOUBLE DOGHOUSE

and then over the .

TWIN MOUNTAINS

At the  we see a puppy.

DOUBLE DOGHOUSE

He is stuck inside!

 **BOOTS** will try to open the **DOOR**.
The  **DOOR** does not open.

In English we say "open."

In Spanish we say "abre."

 says "Abre!"

BOOTS

The  opens.

DOOR

The puppy is free.

The puppy has a twin!

Off we go to the  .
TWIN MOUNTAINS

The look too steep
TWIN MOUNTAINS

to climb.

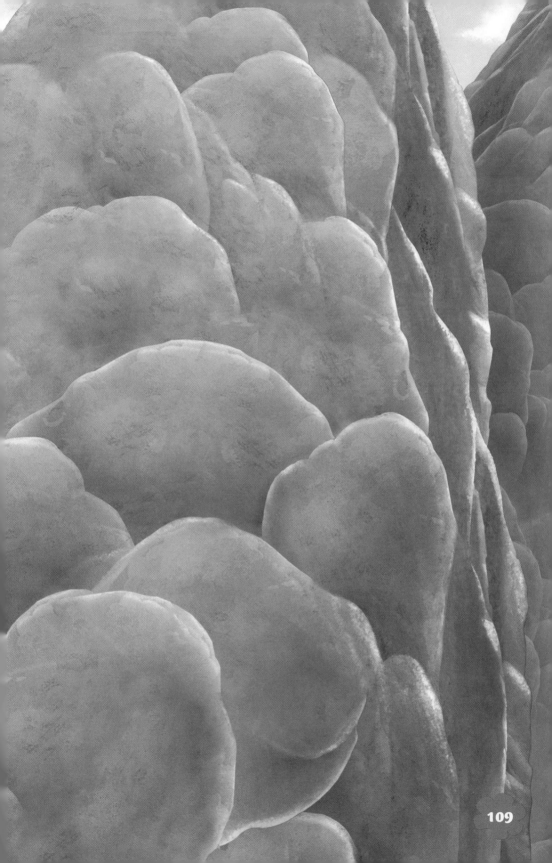

Look! Here come our friends  and !

JOHAN   FRANZ

They have a and .

ROPE   HARNESSES

The and can help
ROPE   HARNESSES

us!

We all grab the  and .

ROPE   HARNESSES

Up, up, up we climb.

At the top we see a  SLIDE .

Down we go.

We are almost at the .

PARTY

But  is tired.

PERRITO

He needs an energy .

BISCUIT

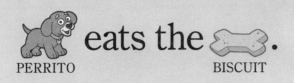 eats the .

PERRITO   BISCUIT

Now he is ready!

Off we go to the .

PARTY

I see my  FAMILY ! But  PERRITO

cannot find his twin.

We need to match up

all the twins.

Will you help us?

It worked!  found

his twin brother.

Oh, no! We see !

PERRITO

SWIPER

Is he trying to swipe that ?

DOG TOY

Oh! SWIPER did not come

to swipe something.

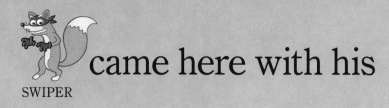 SWIPER came here with his

own puppy! And that

puppy is  PERRITO 's twin!

DORA the EXPLORER®

Dora's Sleepover

by Lara Bergen
illustrated by Victoria Miller

Hi! I am 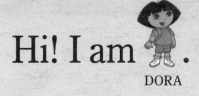.
DORA

It is a big night!

I am having a sleepover with my best friend, ,
BOOTS
at his  !
TREE HOUSE

First I need to pack  .

BACKPACK

Do you see what I should

pack?

I will take my ,
PAJAMAS

my , my ,
FLASHLIGHT   SLEEPING BAG

and my of stories.
BOOK   PIRATE

loves stories!

BOOTS PIRATE

MAMI has made some **COOKIES**

for **BOOTS** and me. Yum!

MAMI puts the **COOKIES**

in a **BASKET**.

Do **you** like 🍪 ?
COOKIES

Thank you, 🧍‍♀️ .
MAMI

Good-bye!

How do we get
to 's BOARD TREE HOUSE ?

BOOTS   TREE HOUSE

MAP can show us

the way.

We go through the ,
TUNNEL

then through the ,
JUNGLE

and that's how we get to

's .

BOOTS   TREE HOUSE

We made it to the  .

TUNNEL

But the  is **so** dark!

TUNNEL

132

Is there something

in my 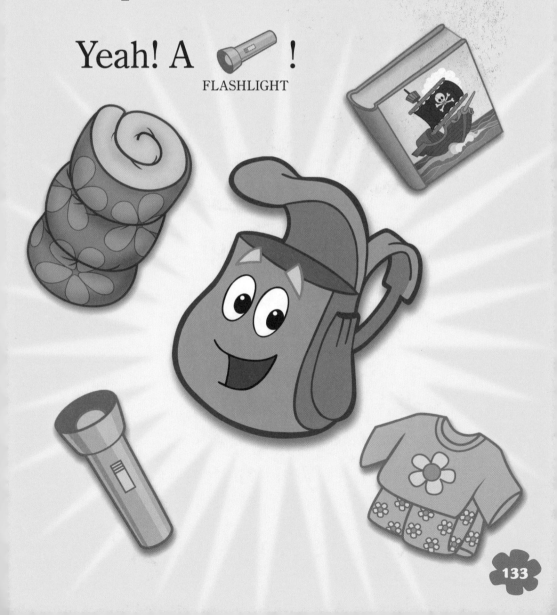 BACKPACK that will

help us see in the dark?

Yeah! A FLASHLIGHT !

We made it through the .
TUNNEL

Now we need to go

through the .
JUNGLE

Uh-oh! Do you see

someone behind that ?
TREE

It is !
SWIPER

 wants to swipe our
SWIPER

 of .
BASKET   COOKIES

Say " , no swiping!"
SWIPER

135

We stopped .

SWIPER

And there is 's !

BOOTS   TREE HOUSE

We can climb the  LADDER

to get to  's BOOTS  . TREE HOUSE

Hi, BOOTS! I am ready

for our sleepover!

I have my  ,
PAJAMAS

my FLASHLIGHT , my SLEEPING BAG ,

my BOOK of PIRATE stories,

and a BASKET of COOKIES

from MAMI !

139

It is time to put on our .
PAJAMAS

Then we can turn on our

 and eat the .

FLASHLIGHTS   COOKIES

Yum!

I can read my  **BOOK**

of **PIRATE** stories

to **BOOTS** too.

Look at the 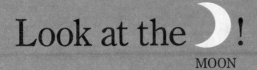!
MOON

The is so big and bright.
MOON

 yawns.
BOOTS

 is sleepy.
BOOTS

142

I am sleepy too.

We get into our .

SLEEPING BAGS

Good night, 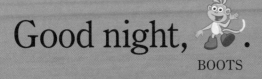.

BOOTS

And good night

to you, too!